MAX & MO's
Science Fair Surprise!

For Margaret "Bunny" Gabel:
As always, your wisdom is at the root of it all.
—Patricia Lakin

For Alfie
—Priscilla Lamont

SIMON SPOTLIGHT
An imprint of Simon & Schuster Children's Publishing Division
1230 Avenue of the Americas, New York, New York 10020
This Simon Spotlight edition May 2020
Text copyright © 2020 by Patricia Lakin
Illustrations copyright © 2020 by Brian Floca
SIMON SPOTLIGHT, READY-TO-READ, and colophon are
registered trademarks of Simon & Schuster, Inc.
For information about special discounts for bulk purchases, please
contact Simon & Schuster Special Sales at 1-866-506-1949
or business@simonandschuster.com.
Manufactured in the United States of America 0320 LAK
2 4 6 8 10 9 7 5 3 1
This book has been cataloged with the Library of Congress.
ISBN 978-1-5344-6322-6 (hc)
ISBN 978-1-5344-6323-3 (pbk)
ISBN 978-1-5344-6324-0 (eBook)

MAX & MO's
Science Fair Surprise!

By Patricia Lakin
Illustrated by Priscilla Lamont
in the style of Brian Floca

Ready-to-Read

Simon Spotlight
New York   London   Toronto   Sydney   New Delhi

Max and Mo were
best friends.

They lived in a cozy cage
in the art room at school.

"What are the big ones
making?" asked Mo.
Max read the sign.
"Posters," said Max.
"For the science fair!"

"We like science!
We can look at their
posters for ideas,"
said Max.

"This poster shows us how
to get out of our cage,"
said Mo.
"We can use our wheel!
You pull. I push!"

PUSH

PULL

SLIDE

Max climbed up and out.

Mo climbed up and out.

Down, down, down they slid.

"I pulled," said Max.

"I pushed," said Mo.

"And we used the ramp!
We are clever hamsters."

"We need a project,"
said Mo.
"What will it be?"
Max wondered.

Mo scratched his chin.
He read another poster.
"How a Plant Grows."

"The book says beans need
water and sun to grow,"
said Max.
"We can try to grow them!"

HOW TO GROW BEANS

YOU WILL NEED:

WATER

SUN

Max looked at the list
of things they would need.
"Cotton? Cups? Beans?
Where can we find them?"

Mo scratched his chin.

He saw a bin.

"Let's dive in!"

"Cotton balls!" cheered Mo.
"Look at my beard!" said Max.
"I have a cup cap," said Mo.
"And beans, too!"

"How can we carry them?"
asked Max.

"They can go in
this lunch box,"
said Mo.

"Now we push,"
said Max.
"Up we go!"

Plink!

Plank!

Plonk!

"I am waiting," said Max.
"I am watching," said Mo.
They waited and watched
and counted.

"Nothing yet," said Max.

A few days later . . .

"I see white roots,"
said Mo.
"I see green shoots,"
said Max.

"Our beans are growing!"
"Now we can make
our poster!"

A few minutes later,
someone picked up the cage.
Bing! Bang! Bong!
Where are we going?
Max and Mo wondered.

"Yay! We are at the
science fair too!"
Max and Mo cheered.
"Science is so much fun!"

Want to make some beans sprout?

Here is what you will need:

1. A grown-up's help
2. A variety of whole dried beans (white or red kidney beans, navy beans, lima beans—not cooked or in a can)
3. Clear plastic cups
4. Cotton balls
5. Water
6. Calendar

Here is what to do:

1. Pack

2. Place near sunlight

3. Water

4. Watch and wait

Want to plant the sprouted beans indoors?
Here is what you will need:

1. A grown-up's help
2. Cardboard egg carton or a milk or juice carton
3. Soil
4. Scissors and tape
5. A metal straw or wooden stirrer
6. Index cards and a pencil

Here is what to do:

1. Plant

2. Water

3. Label the different bean sprouts, and place near sunlight.

4. Watch